The Angle of
Sharpest Ascending

for David Trinidad,
new friend in Chicago,
with appreciation,
Ingrid Wendt
March 2004

The Angle of Sharpest Ascending

Poems by Ingrid Wendt

WordTech Editions

© 2004 by Ingrid Wendt

Published by WordTech Editions, imprint of Word Press
P.O. Box 541106
Cincinnati, OH 45254-1106

ISBN: 1932339-04-3
LCCN: 2003105924

Poetry Editor: Kevin Walzer
Business Editor: Lori Jareo

Typeset in Goudy Old Style BT by WordTech Communications,
Cincinnati, OH

Visit us on the web at www.wordtechweb.com

Visit the author's website at www.ingridwendt.com

Acknowledgments

"Questions of Mercy" was first published in *Nimrod International Journal* as a finalist in the Pablo Neruda Awards.

"Learning the Mother Tongue" first appeared in *Prairie Schooner*.

"Questions of Mercy" and "Learning the Mother Tongue" have appeared as a chapbook, *Blow the Candle Out*, Pecan Grove Press, March 2002.

Grateful acknowledgment is made to Denise Levertov, for permission to use words from her poem "Life at War," and for her encouragement. Deep thanks also to Marilyn Krysl, for permission to quote from her poem "Nammu: To Adam," as well as for her example and encouragement.

I wish also to acknowledge the United States Fulbright Program and the J.W. Goethe University, Frankfurt/Main, Germany, for sponsoring my Senior Fulbright Professorship during academic year 1994-95. The Mary Anderson Center for the Arts, Indiana, provided a residency fellowship during which "Questions of Mercy" was written. Grateful appreciation, also, to the Kulturreferat München for a residency at the Villa Waldbeta, Feldafing, Germany, as well as to the University of Oregon departments of German, Fine Arts, and International Studies, the Center for the Study of Women in Society, the Oregon Humanities Center, and the Jewish Student Union, for their support of the interdisciplinary exhibit "Memory/Memorial," held in June 1999, in Eugene, Oregon.

Special gratitude to visual artists Susi Rosenberg, Munich, Germany, who conceived the title "Memory/Memorial"; to Traude Linhardt, Munich, Germany; and to Ingeborg Kolar, Covallis, Oregon. Without their tremendous talents, their hard work, their friendship, and their commitment to our interdisciplinary projects, this book, in its present shape, would not exist. Heartfelt thanks, also, to the Hesse family: Günter, Mechthild and Anna, friends for more than twenty years, who have often shared with me and my family their home, their hearts, and their inside knowledge of German life today. Sonja Lührmann-Vinkovetsky, former student, Ph.D. candidate at the University of Michigan, was my constant, brilliant advisor, offering invaluable perspectives on parts of these poems that led to significant revisions. This book would be less balanced without her.

Everlasting love and thanks to my husband, Ralph Salisbury, who was my good partner in travel; who kept house during times of my absence, with never once a complaint; whose faith in me and in my work has always been constant; who has been my sounding board and, always, my first and best reader; whose own unflinching and uncompromising fidelity to truthfulness, in his life and in his own work, has been my steady example all these many years of our long and blessed marriage.

*This book is dedicated, with love, to the grandparents I never knew
and to the memory of my parents,
Matilda Helen Kathryn Petzke Wendt (1911–2000)
and Edward Julius Wendt (1902–1986)*

*and with joy in being able
(helped by living abroad, by extended family, friends, and German language study)
to overcome my quiet resistance to "German ways" of thinking and doing*

*to learn from my mother, during her last year on earth, the German prayers
of her childhood, which she had continued (without my knowledge) to say
every single day of her life,*

*and to have happy and loving conversations with her, in German,
for the very first time.*

*I dedicate this book also to the German friends, family, and strangers
who told me their stories. Their spiritual burdens became my own.
May this book do them justice.*

We seek to do justice to the suffering without perpetuating the hatred aroused.
Without memory, there is no healing. Without forgiveness, there is no future.
—Archbishop Desmond Tutu

For us, forgetting was never an option.
Remembering is a noble and necessary act.
—Elie Wiesel

Competitive suffering is not the way to advance compassion.
—Ingrid de Kok

An ear, disjointed, eavesdrops.
An eye, cut into stripes,
does justice to all.
—Paul Celán

You can not step twice into the same river,
for other waters are continually flowing on.
It is in changing that things find repose.
—Heraclitus, Fragments 21, 23

When the center of someone's life has been blown out like the core of a building,
is it any wonder if it takes so long even to find a door to close?
—Ellen Goodman

Contents

Introduction

Born in the last year of the second world war to parents who had grown up speaking German with their families in Michigan and Chile, but who did not speak it in our Illinois home, I did not, until adolescence, begin to wonder why. "We didn't want you using German words at school," my mother once said. That was it. The issue was closed. But something unspoken, something troubling, stayed with me, waiting to be someday acknowledged and understood. Something involving Germany's role in the second world war, which never, in my memory, was mentioned all the years I was living at home. Perhaps the writing of these poems has been, in part, a way of discovering, and coming to terms with, the rest of what my parents were not able to say.

As a child I intuited something else, something about the connection between the German language and the values and folkways with which I was raised, and, as an adolescent and young adult I put great energy into differentiating myself from my family, as young people do. Despite my love of the brothers Grimm, of castles, Beethoven, and küchen, despite having taken pride—as a small child—in learning a handful of German words, as a young adult I rejected the German language, saying, as I'd heard others say, it sounded ugly, it had too many rules, it was hard to learn. Not until 1983, when I was making plans to live in Germany for several months, did

I make any serious effort to put aside my dislike of the language, and try to learn enough to "get by." Many more years had to pass before I could write "Learning the Mother Tongue," the poem with which this book begins.

But "Learning the Mother Tongue" was not the first of these four to be written. Several triggering events took place in 1995, in the Spring of the deeply instructive year I spent as a Senior Fulbright Professor at the University of Frankfurt on Main.

Good friends, fluent in English, were taking me on a Sunday afternoon jaunt to visit the grounds of an ancient, crumbling, ivy-covered monastery about an hour's drive from home. The day was rainy, but that didn't seem to matter to my friends or to the several dozen other tourists, all of them German, as we explored walkways and cloisters, admiring the picturesque decay of the walls and the carvings on ancient, faded tombs. One spot puzzled me: what were those small, unmarked, rectangles of brass in the central courtyard? My friends were vague: some kind of graves, maybe, they said. That made sense. I thought no further.

The next day—through startling coincidence—I found out more. Arriving early at the high school where I was to be a guest speaker, I read a bulletin board and discovered that the students had—just the week before—done a lengthy report, in English as well as in German, complete with photos from a recent newspaper story, about the same courtyard I had just visited. It was the burial place for 88 prison factory workers, men and women, massacred by the SS during the German retreat from advancing American troops, 50 years before.

I was overcome by rage, a rage so powerful I barely calmed down in time for class. Rage returned in full force when class was done. But at whom—at what—was I angry? At the irony of fate? We Americans were the liberators! At my friends, maybe, for not telling the whole truth? Of course (reason told me), they might not have known. But there'd been a long, explanatory sign, in German, near the courtyard; I'd seen them reading it. I felt betrayed. And filled with terrible guilt.

I wrote about this event in my journal, and reread it, the following September, along with other journal entries, during a three-week writing residency at Indiana's Mary Anderson Center for the Arts. I found I'd recorded, at different times of the year, the personal stories of several middle-aged Germans—strangers, family, friends—about the second world war: stories of air raid shelters; of playing hide and seek in the rubble; of bodies, hunger, and cold; of families fleeing the advancing Russian troops. One recurring theme was the shock of learning, in later childhood, the full extent of what their country had done, and the fear that soldier fathers, who had been killed or had returned from being prisoners of war, might have done unspeakable things. Grandparents had sent these fathers to war, had been members of the Nazi party, or, at the least, had not stopped horrors from happening. Pain, grief, and shame—for country, for family—have still not gone away, and have been experienced by virtually everyone born in Germany during and shortly after the war, including my good, jaunt-loving friends.

Re-reading my journal accounts of these conversations, I found myself unexpectedly, and often, in tears: my mourning, like my earlier rage, inexplicable. At that point there was no question of remaining a listener. "Questions of Mercy" began to take shape.

I remember one of my college instructors, years ago, pointing out that the word "compassion" has at its root the Latin "*compati*: suffer with." I do not intend, ever, to diminish the horrors of the second world war and of the deaths of 6 million—Jews, homosexuals, the disabled, dissidents, gypsies—in the Holocaust. I hope I never fail to acknowledge the rage and grief of survivors. I believe in the importance of the scholarship, the art, the writing that have been going on for over fifty years, demanding: How could this have happened? I believe it is of vital importance that coming generations learn this part of history, that it not disappear.

I also believe in the importance—for the future safety of our country, our world— of trying to understand how perpetrators of violence can do violence to themselves, can be victims of wrong teaching, of mass hysteria, of propaganda. To recognize that evil can be taught.

Two years ago, in 2001, New York City's Jewish Museum held a controversial exhibit titled "Mirroring Evil: Nazi Imagery/Recent Art." A departure from most previous art about the Holocaust, which has focused primarily on images of victims, the works in this courageous exhibit dared to explore the world and the psyches of the perpetrators, and focused on a wide range of images used in the Nazi "propaganda machine"—images which bear unsettling resemblance, as the exhibit clearly demonstrated, to images by which we in America are every day surrounded, and to whose presence most of us are blind.

Poet Alice Derry, in an eloquent introduction to her book *Strangers to Their Courage*, quotes Michael Blumenthal, whose words bear repeating: "There is a certain easy solace, I fear, in labeling one crime ... as history's 'worst,' one people as history's most egregious villains. It allows the rest of us ... to be subjected to a lower standard of morality, to enjoy an easier sleep." Carefully documenting her facts, Derry takes a position similar to Blumenthal's:

> While the present generation of Germans ... is still often made to feel the guilt which rightly belongs to their parents or grandparents, many Americans don't see that the same accusations can be applied to them. ... Ample documentation exists to show that the Allies knew of the Jews' suffering, and—beyond the help of a few private agencies like the Quakers—did nothing to prevent it. As Americans now know to our shame, whatever the official stance, our State department worked secretly to keep Jewish refugees out of the U.S. ... What happened in Germany was not an isolated event.

And with regard to the history of violence within my own country, am I, as an American, more immune than my German friends, colleagues, and extended family to inherited guilt and shame? Or is my country simply better at forgetting? Am I not living in a country that enjoys the bounties of a land that was taken—at horrible human cost, and not too long ago—from those who lived here before me? Several years ago, while editing *From Here We Speak: An Anthology of Oregon Poetry*, I found pioneer poets who gloried in the wonders of a land they felt their rightful gift from God, but I also discovered that within the borders of this state once lived over 40 different tribal nations, with over 20 distinct languages, all but erased by systematic genocide. Native Americans are not the only group to have suffered socially-acceptable violence at the hands of founding Americans. As Oregon poet Patricia McLean has recently written, "Members of my family came to this continent in the 1500s and in the course of time ... were part of the evil of slave ownership. I am sure they thought they were good people. That is what is so frightening. ... I know that whatever privilege I have as a white American is due to the suffering of others."

In her book *Small Wonder*, Barbara Kingsolver writes: "I am losing faith in such a simple thing as despising an enemy with unequivocal righteousness. A mirror held up to every moral superiority will show its precise mirror image: The terrorist loves his truth as hard as I love mine; he has a mother who looks on her child with the same fierce pride I feel when I look at my own." In this world, where wars continue to follow one another as regularly and almost as predictably as the seasons, where the justifiable hatreds aroused by the horrible acts of one group, one country, are handed down by survivors to successive generations, as the memory of the massacre of Serbs at Kosovo Polje, in 1389, is presented as reason to fight today—is it possible for us to learn compassion not only for war's victims but for its perpetrators, whose monumental human failures could, just possibly, mirror our own? Can cycles of hatred ever be broken without all of us, citizens of the world, learning to imagine ourselves in the stead of all who suffer—even when those who suffer have brought it on themselves? Can peace be within our reach when victors continue to think themselves superior to those they defeat?

While films such as *Schindler's List* and novels such as Ursula Hegi's *Stones in the River* show us there were, in fact, ordinary German citizens who acted with courage, and at great personal risk, to save whomever they could, what is less commonly known, here in America, is the effort being made by many of today's Germans to come to grips with their past. Until fairly recently, what writer Ursula Hegi documented in *Tearing the Silence*, a book of interviews with German American immigrants after the war, was disturbingly true: German parents and grandparents, who lived through the war, who were part of the war, maintained an almost-incomprehensible silence about it, never processing what should have been a deep sense of guilt and grief for acts committed and permitted.

With younger generations, however, things have been changing. I think of the traveling exhibit I saw in downtown Frankfurt, in 1997: the one demonstrating, in hundreds of never-before collected photographs from the attics of German soldiers and the families of these soldiers, the degree of involvement of the regular German army, the *Wehrmacht*, in atrocities against dissidents and Jews. True, some German cities—Munich among them—refused to allow this exhibit a public venue. But the overwhelming, record attendance in Frankfurt, as well as in many other German cities, was clear evidence of a need to confront, to process, to come to terms. I think of the exhibit *"Politea"* I saw in the Women's Museum in Bonn: frank, stark photographs of the after-war years in Germany, and women's role in rebuilding—physically, as well as economically—a new, viable society from the rubble. I think of the monuments, all over Germany, in train stations, in town squares, alongside walls, acknowledging the horrors that occurred there. I am encouraged by these things. As Derry rightly says, "...only to the degree to which ordinary Germans can come to terms with their own past and their parents' and grandparents' pasts by being openly honest about what really happened and living in full acceptance of it can psychic health be restored in their country. On our small planet the health of one nation is part of the health of all nations."

Until my friends, colleagues, and extended German family told me their stories, I had thought very little of what could have been my own experience, had my Chilean father not, in 1929, left Germany, where he had been working for two years, and come to the United States to learn English to further his career in the import-export business, and, ultimately, to marry and live the rest of his life. Until I visited, late in my Fulbright year, a German war cemetery in France, in the Alsace region, in a small town close to the Rhine, I had given no thought to what kind of burial sites had been accorded the German war dead. Familiar with images of Arlington National Cemetery, and of the enormous graveyards of the fallen in Belgium and France, I was expecting the opposite here: random gravestones overgrown with grasses and weeds, and tended by benign neglect. This was the enemy, after all.

What I found, instead, shook me. Thousands of identical white crosses, covering the hilltop in geometrically perfect, intersecting planes. Neatly mown grass, maintained by a multi-national, European youth organization. A visitor's room with an enormous guest book, filled with German-language entries. Reading them, I became overwhelmed by emotion, and could not stay—not knowing that several months later this experience would, in recollection, become the concluding section of "Questions of Mercy."

The three other long poems in this book—none of which were even begun for another two years; none of which would have been written without "Questions of Mercy" leading the way—had their origins in less dramatic circumstances. Correspondence and a growing friendship with Munich sculptor Susi Rosenberg, whom I'd met at the Frankfurt Art Fair in 1995, led to our receiving, two years later, a stipend from the Cultural Ministry of Munich to work together for the month of April 1997, with Munich painter Traude Linhardt, at the Villa Waldberta: a small, state-run artists' community on Lake Starnberg, just south of Munich. We chose the theme for our collaboration, "Space : Word : Time," well in advance. Once we were together at the Villa, this theme led us into intense, daily discussions about how we perceived the various intersections of those abstractions, and then we'd retire to our studios to work on our separate, yet related, artworks: mine, the creation of "Suite for the Spirit's Geometry," (as well as—unexpectedly—the outline and beginnings of "Learning the Mother

Tongue"); Linhardt's, a monumental painting/installation titled "Time Stations;" and Rosenberg's, two large freestanding sculptures: "*Gestörtes Wachtum*: Interrupted Growth" and "Path I," all of which are described at the end of this book.

Different from anything I'd ever written before, both in content and in the process of creation, "Suite for the Spirit's Geometry" arose through our collaboration in at least three main ways. One, with regard to form: the poem, paintings, and sculptures consisted of many, almost-parallel, repeating sections, with variations in content from section to section. Two: poem, paintings, and sculptures were all manifestations of the same theme: the relation between and intersection of time, word, and space, as perceived in our personal and shared histories. Three: the images in each artwork were preceded by concepts, rather than the other way around. For someone who was used to beginning with image, with concrete experience, and to using the act of writing to see what concepts might emerge, this new "backward" way of working was a particularly difficult, and rewarding, challenge.

Shortly after returning home to Eugene, Oregon, I discovered a photography installation by Corvallis artist Ingeborg Kolar: a memorial to her father, a medical doctor lost at sea in a German submarine. This led me to envision a new, three-part project: an interdisciplinary art exhibit with Kolar, Rosenberg (whose mother is an Auschwitz survivor) and myself. Two years of preparations for "Memory/Memorial" included securing funds from six University of Oregon departments to bring Rosenberg to Eugene for a three-month period in Spring of 1999, and extensive long-distance correspondence with both Kolar and Rosenberg. We read and discussed some of the same books, among them Susan Griffin's *A Chorus of Stones*; Eric Santner's *Stranded Objects: Mourning, Memory, and Film in Postwar Germany*; Harriet Epstein's *Children of the Holocaust*; Ursula Hegi's *Tearing the Silence*, and James Young's *The Texture of Memory: Holocaust Memorials and Meaning*. We attended a lecture by James Young, at the University of Oregon, and another by Arthur Kleinman.

During this time of preparation I was especially alert to current issues involving the construction of public memorials in various parts of the world: debates about the future Berlin Holocaust memorial; images of women in the Vietnam War memorials; the *My Lai* Peace Park Project; the work to create a National Tribal Memorial Park at Wounded Knee; plans for memorializing the victims of the Oklahoma City bombing; the recent unveiling of the ValueJet memorial in the Everglades; the fence around Thurston High School in Springfield, Oregon, just across the river from my home in Eugene, with flowers turning to brown, and plans to construct a memorial which would/would not include the names of the young, cafeteria gunman's parents, whom he had killed, as well. These were painful times. The attacks of 9/11/01 had not yet occurred, but the list was long, and the issues surrounding each memorial project were complex.

Patterns of concerns began to emerge: the impossibility of redemption versus hope of reconciliation; issues of restorative justice; of how to reclaim, through memorializing, a sense of dignity and self worth, beyond material reparations. The need to honor those lost to us, to acknowledge their suffering, to establish places where mourning can occur, where memory can be kept alive. The question of whether these places should also instruct.

At every turn I found myself with more questions than answers. At what point does memory become memorial? What memories do we choose and which choose us? Which personal images speak for others? Can we revise images from the past to reflect the values of today? Whose values? Moreover, how do we choose to harness the power of memory to ennoble or to destroy? The moment of the "slash," the point of balance and stasis, the moment of change, became central to all parts of the poem, "Suite for 'Memory/Memorial'," I wrote for this exhibit.

Rather than an attempt to answer questions, this poem became a partial reconstruction of moments of coming to awareness: of steps on the complex path of connecting my own personal sense of memory/memorial with what these words mean to others here at home, in other parts of the world, and in the land of my grandparents.

My hope is that this book, as a whole, will reach beyond the borders of its origin. That the pathway of its thoughts will also be its own form of memorial, honoring the nature of our human condition and the memories each of us brings to this moment today. May you who read these lines find places where they speak for you.

For Further Exploration

Amichai, Yehuda. "Who Will Remember the Rememberers?" Poem. *The New Republic*, 20 December 1999. 38-39.

Derry, Alice. *Strangers to Their Courage*. Poems. Baton Rouge: Louisiana State University Press, 2001.

Dobler, Patricia. *UXB*. Original poems and translations of poems by Ilse Aichinger. Pittsburgh: Mill Hunk Books, 1991.

Forché, Carolyn. *The Angel of History*. Poems. New York: HarperCollins, 1994.

Epstein, Harriet. *Children of the Holocaust: Conversations with Sons and Daughters of Survivors*. New York: Putnam, 1979.

Frauen Museum. *Politeia: Szenarien Aus Der Deutschen Geschichte Nach 1945 Aus Frauensicht*. Exhibition catalog and essays. Prof. Dr. Annette Kuhn, Marianne Pitzen, Marianne Hochgeschurz, editors. Bonn: Siering, 1998.

Goldhagen, Daniel. *Hitler's Willing Executioners: Ordinary Germans and the Holocaust*. New York: Knopf, 1996.

Griffin, Susan. *A Chorus of Stones: the Private Life of War*. New York: Doubleday, 1992.

Hamburger Institut für Sozialforschung. *Vernichtungskrieg. Verbrechen der Wehrmacht 1941 bis 1944*. Exhibition catalog. Christian Reuther and Johannes Bacher, editors. Hamburg: Hamburger Edition HIS Verlagsges. mbH

Hegi, Ursula. *Stones from the River*. Novel. New York: Simon and Schuster, 1994.

_____. *Tearing the Silence.* Interviews. New York: Simon and Schuster, 1997.

Hirschfield, Ted. *German Requiem: Poems of the War and the Atonement of a Third Reich Child.* Poems. Saint Louis, Missouri: Time Being Books, 1993.

Kingsolver, Barbara. *Small Wonder.* Essays. New York: HarperCollins, 2002.

Kleeblatt, Norman L., Editor. *Mirroring Evil: Nazi Imagery/Recent Art.* Essays. New York and New Brunswick: The Jewish Museum and Rutgers University Press, 2002.

MacLean, Patricia. Personal correspondence with Ingrid Wendt, 22 May 2003.

McGeary, Johanna. "Echoes of the Holocaust." *Time,* 24 February 1997, 37-40. (Other articles in this issue, on Nazi gold in Switzerland: Thomas Sancton, "A Painful History," 40-44, and Lance Morrow, "The Justice of the Calculator, 45.)

Osherow, Jacqueline. *Conversations with Survivors.* Poems. Athens, Georgia: University of Georgia Press, 1994.

Rabinowitz, Anna. *Darkling.* Book-length poem. Dorset, VT: Tupelo Press, 2001.

Santner, Eric L. *Stranded Objects: Mourning, Memory, and Film in Postwar Germany.* Essays. Ithaca, New York: Cornell University Press, 1990.

Schjeldahl, Peter. "The Good German: Gerhard Richter's Triumphant Sorrow." *The New Yorker,* 4 March 2002, 84-85.

_____. "The Hitler Show: The Jewish Museum Revisits the Nazis." *The New Yorker*, 1 April 2002, 87.

Schlink, Bernhard. *The Reader*. Novel. New York: Vintage International, Random House, 1998.

Thiel, Diane. *Echolocations*. Poems. Ashland, Oregon: Story Line Press, 2000.

Wichin, Harriet, director. *Silent Witness*. Documentary film. 16 mm, color. Canada. German with English subtitles. 74 min. 1994.

Young, James. *The Texture of Memory: Holocaust Memorials and Meaning*. New Haven: Yale University Press, 1993.

I.

LEARNING THE MOTHER TONGUE

1.

It's wicked, I know, but sometimes I can't help feeling just
the tiniest glee when my good German friend, whose English tongue
has mastered the footwork of all Swan Lake ballet, stumbles over
the English translation of *wenn*, saying "if" when she really means
"when," and vice versa,

                     while I, good German American, keep
clumping along: learning the word *Kopfsalat*, for example ("head
lettuce"), so proud of myself: first time in the land of all four
grandparents, shopping for salad, asking the produce clerk "*Haben Sie
ein Kopf, bitte?*" "*Ja, natürlich,*" she answers. "*Und Sie?*"

2.

But this is what comes of book learning, not every day stretching
the tongue: discipline, discipline, flash cards, syllables
splashing in and out of the ear

out of context: out of their forests
of kelp: circling, circling, whole
words unbidden as fragments of tunes

Denkbar, I hear, and it's one of those reef fish floating up
to my face mask, right out of my fish classification book
but right then the name won't come, I have to look it up

Ergebnis, I hear, (outcome/result)
Abgeschiedenheit (solitude): listen
what am I telling myself, and in whose voice?

3.

"Brr," I practice, over and over, the special teacher so happy
(so easy to please), "Brr, Brr, Brr, Brrd" (such a pretty
poster: blue jays, orioles, robins) and then
we blow the candle out. Not

with lips puckered, oh no, that's the usual way,
but because I am special, this secret: the tongue
not behind the teeth ("Duh"), but rather just
a flicker beneath: "Thhh, Thhh, Thhh," the breath

we can chase with another nice sound: "The," "They," "This,"
"That." Six years old. And two weeks later I master what
my German-Chilean father, with more than twenty years in this country,
whose accent has read to me to sleep each night from the moment

books began, still
hasn't achieved.

4.

Always the question: Did our Illinois family speak German at home?
During the war years in which I was born? Let's qualify:

Father born 1902 in Chile. Mother, 1911, in Michigan. There, that does it.
Except for the shadow. *(Fit in. Fit in. What else is there to know?)*

5.

And still, "*Mach schnell!*" (when I was too slow).
"*Strewwelpeter!*" (my hair was a mess).
"*Dreh dich rum,*" my mother would say in her Schwabian mother's

tongue, never, of course, outside of the family, never
translating: sporadic spices her tongue dished out without
one of us questioning. Look!

In this textbook, the recipes: words with real
meanings attached. "Make quick!" "Naughty
child from Heinrich Hoffmann's pen!" It's not

after all, just
family oddness, not
baby talk. Look at

this middle-aged tongue abandon its teetering. This
fabulous, sturdy new foot!

6.

Yet what translation for what wasn't spoken?

A child's duty is following orders, no questions. A leader is bad, if he fails.
Parents are always, always, always right. You've had your fun. Now, duty.

Where this came from, what child thought to ask? She knew.

7.

Ach, this relentlessness. *Ach*, this unforgiving
side of the tongue. "*Grübeleien*," the German-American poet
Ted Hirschfield calls it. "The German search for perfect order."

(Good, better, best. Never let it rest, till the good
is better, and the better, best.) Meaning: Good is never
good enough. Good is always one step backwards into bad.

Which maybe has something to do with "Case": the ways all nouns
can be rearranged (*Who* does *What* to *Whom*, unpredictable):
lacking the right "the," you can say something strange:

The mother gives the girl a spanking.
The girl gives the mother a spanking.
The spanking gives the girl to the mother.

Not *Why*, of course.
Never *Why*.

8.

Why did the father never
punish the child? Why let the mother
shoulder all anger? All

those years the child thinking her father the most
perfect: the one she failed to please the one
time and one time only, all

the years of her childhood the one time she asked him
to teach her German and he raised his voice in such fire
as never could issue forth from him and all

because she could not pronounce no matter
how many times she tried, the "*ü*" umlaut he over and over
tried to teach her and over and over all

her stubby, graceless tongue could muster was "*oo.*"

9.

CASE (n.)

Covering. (Middle English, *case*; Old French, *casse*; Latin, *capsa:*
        carton, from *capere:* to hold)

Situation. (Middle English, *case*; Old French, *cas:* event, chance;
        Latin, *casus:* accident, from *cadere:* to fall)

Condition/state/circumstance/
plight/
predicament

10.

And who in those days in her hearing said one word about World War II

11.

What cannot be spoken
What cannot be heard
Sharp instant of knowing
No substitute word

For a meaning uncharted
Beyond either tide
Bridge between continents
Dateline Divide

What pulses on paper
Precarious heart
Could break like a wave
Could wash us apart

Still moment of tension
License to choose
And/or/something more
History/News

Silent as footsteps
That cannot be sung
What will not be recognized
Severs the tongue

12.

Gang: way of walking.

Vergangen: bygone, former, last, past.

Vergangenheit: our history.

Vergären: curdle; to ferment.

Vergänglich: passing; transient.

Wal: whale.

Walten: to prevail.

Bewalden: plant with trees.

Bewährung: security.

Bewältigen: to cope.

Vergangenheitsbewältigung: to come
to terms with the past; regroup.

13.

To know who we are. To speak. To start all over again, lugging along the whole
sense of everything, all that kit and kaboodle, not only the meanings of nouns,
verbs, adjectives, but

the structure of speech itself: planning the order of each
sentence
a rucksack of rations the mind

carries along on its everyday field maneuvers. Such
a burden of foreknowledge. Such earnest
syllables: look again: "the"

can never be just "the," it's *die*, or *der*, or *das*, and
depending on where in the sentence you find it, *dem* or *den*,
and don't forget "number," *des*, and maybe this verb or that

preposition takes dative or genitive case, O, the combinations
would baffle even the periodic table of elements. You could be
forever held in suspension: before you can open your mouth,

the solution must always, always, always be at sentence end already
known. That slap you never knew was coming. No end to the blame
you (or she) (or he) (or we) could own.

14.

To believe we are what we speak, and still take
heart: how

about the implications of "*Art*"
("nature") and "*artig*"
("well-behaved")?

And how do you like these words, like Chinese ideograms, pictures
to cling to: *Selbständig*, ("self-standing;"
"independent").

Unabhängig, ("not hanging on;" "independent").
Hochfliegen, ("high-flying;"
"explode").

15.

Abgeschiedenheit, O you syllables rolling
over the palate: thick milkshake: such work to
pull you through the straw, such dense reward

Sehenswürdigkeit (sight worth seeing), O you rich
stew with your stock ingredients—garlic, carrots, celery,
onions, beans—look at your infinite mutations!

Wiedersehen
Wiederaufnameverfahren
Kinderfreundsehenlichkeit

(We can even make some of these up) and even
the singular ones, the peppercorns, how sweet to the tongue:
nein, the mother says to her little one

gentle, this sound the moon
makes when it's full—the lap, the pillow—not
"No," not "*Nyet,*" but *nein, nein, nein.*

16.

And the other side of meaning's suspension: all
the sweetness of cookie dough: this isn't the end, the best's

Yet to come. All
the intellectual passion of Wagner, of *Tristan, Isolde.*

The consummate pleasure of consummation withheld. All
this intricate, verbal footwork: words like chess pieces:

Langsam, deliberate, *langsam,* slowly. This *Tango.*
Flamenco.

This power.
Control.

17.

"Bist du

ein gutes Mädchen?"

"Ja, ich bin ein gutes Mädchen."

Out of hiding, this memory, that morning. I'm ten. This whole
sentence I say again and again, snuggling, Saturday morning and
Mother letting us under her covers, into the words she learned from her

own mother: words I learn by rote, not sense, but now, here
in this class, with this text, in one big bang, the whole
hump of Africa—foothold

every map of Europe stands on—sliding back
into the lap of Florida, Mexico, Texas, where once it belonged:
gutes (*natürlich*): predicate nominative (how

logical) intersecting with singular neuter (you've got it): one small part
        of the whole ballet
my tongue will learn (*natütrlich*) from what the runaway heart
brings home.

II.

SUITE FOR THE SPIRIT'S GEOMETRY

Part of the interdisciplinary artwork titled "Time: Word: Space," first shown

at the Villa Waldberta, Feldafing, Germany, April 26–27, 1997

For Susi Rosenberg, sculptor and Traude Linhardt, painter

OVERTURE

"All art aspires to the condition of music."

—Schopenhauer

I, too, love
spatial constructions: together we speak
      of tension, counterpoint, play
         of word on word, the spirit's

geometry: time, space, paths of
memory, interrupted
      growth and all of the past
layered: what else

pulls at us? What

rhythms? Each
physical space
      with its own
         implications:

the structure of language reflecting
all of its inner

assumptions: German,
American, my

own feet the points of a compass
straddling oceans:

the force of the four-line stanza,
opposed to three; the spirit
soaring in verticals;
opening, closing in arches

broken, resurrected in steel, what

concrete parallels, train tracks,
what real things from our lives?

2.

Or is it possible? Images, are they reliable?

Everyone knows the story: the fish
each time we tell it, inflating:
minnow to whale.

Song lyrics mutating one
word for another with each mountain they cross,
each river: whole new hybrids of meaning. My father

the time he sneezed and his false teeth went flying
across the parking lot, under the car, laughing with us a bit
more with each telling, his stardom growing from twinkle to blaze.

3.

And isn't this also Axiom: changes too
small for recognition: that part in the hair for years
relentlessly centered, edging towards the right side of the head, how
does this happen? The hair a little shorter, each time it's cut. The sweaters we
fold and stack in the wardrobe: green on the left, always, grey on the right, but one day
(how did that happen?) the order's

                        reversed. The socks you walked
away with and put somewhere you can't remember.
The letter misplaced. The keys. Your feet
have you noticed? will find them for you.
Let them retrace where they've been.
This meter of your body. It knows.

4.

And what of those memories seeming
never to change, echoing: broken
records: words not spoken; the one
word that can't be taken back.

And what postulates for images all of us think we have buried?
Ungoverned, our windmills of memory bring them up to the surface
again and again: the girl on the campus green, kneeling over the
classmate inexplicably dead; the naked child running

forever towards us, burning in napalm; the place you remember
being, exactly, and what you were doing the moment you heard
your leader was shot. How you passed the time
until he was dead.

5.

As though Time were something tangible.

As though Time gave us something predictable.

As though Time treated each image the same.

6.

Transgress
Transport
Transplant
Transmute
Transfuse
Transpire
Transform
Transcend

7.

Unwritten, still, this theorem: the same
daffodils I plant in early December will bloom the same
week as those in the yard of my neighbors who faithfully
plant on time: October, at latest.

This counterpoint: forty-five onetime classmates brought
hundreds of miles together for three hours one October
evening, all of them born in the very same year,
no two of them equally grown-up, mature.

8.

And just as predictable: rugs again and again pulled
out from under today. Where is our footing? All (for example)
these Munich parkways, so wide! (I say) compared to Frankfurt.
Such airy, green spaces in front of the arch!

Yes, that's where good King Ludwig ordered whole
neighborhoods leveled (she tells me). This green: it covers
the concrete where Hitler made speeches, held rallies, it's one of
the first places books were burned.

9.

Break

Separate

Isolate

Sort

Group

Cluster

Gather

Harvest

10.

If all art forms have something in common, perhaps
it is this: between conception

and resolution

between the vision (consummate,
this flower garden) and

our names for it (iris, lily, gardenia, rose)

this interval: space and time in one
simultaneous burst of connection, and look

how much time it takes to tell it, what

linear order to put everything in?

Eyes, feet, wanting a
path to follow; logic, expecting
beginning, middle and end, with some

kind of suspense, some climax, some reason to keep
going forward as though revelation will bloom at the end.

Mozart, it's said, saw his symphonies whole. Complete.
Outlines of movements like ribs of the skeleton, spine

of the fish, the leaf, the bare branches of trees in the forest.

The whole forest in song. Like that.
He wrote down the notes. He fleshed it all in.

11.

These words, how much time it takes to read them!

12.

Everything connects: chance meetings across
years and hundreds of miles: fractals of waves and the
cast off industrial wastes. Paintings. Sculptures. Steel and concrete.
Slivers of glass, the sand it has come from returning
back to itself. Rust blossoms on train tracks, let us
help it along. Paint crumbles, books
curl and disintegrate.

Tenderly let us
recognize all parts of memory, what we have been given, what we
would rather deny, tenderly let us lay them to rest. Just today
I found a new book of poems, the table of contents ordered
most recent to past: reverse climax: the poet knowing
Everything we are has brought us to this place.
Let us know this and go on.

CODA: RUNE

For every word there is another side
For every grain of sand, a mountain
Rings of trees, the circlings of the tide
For every past a circle to be broken

And we, avoiding all that silent space
Our cryptic memories have formed: what binds
Us to this present moment, here, by grace?
What armors made of wax? Grave tokens?

We, whose footsteps mark the way of time
As though there were but one true clock
One measure of our lives, one common rhyme
What voices of the past have we not chosen?

Scraps of cloth, of stone and wood and steel
Paths between the grains of sand, the mountain
Every turning of the line into the wheel
Every past a silence to be spoken.

III.

QUESTIONS OF MERCY

We are the humans,...who can make;

whose language imagines mercy,

lovingkindness; *we have believed one another*

mirrored forms of a God we felt as good...

—Denise Levertov

1.

Affectionate, almost, the way it is written,
the book of German customs
lent by a friend

the recognition behind
this cartoon: a woman

in kerchief and apron, upright
the vacuum she holds in her hand.

Around her, the rubble:
the building
in ruins, the city in ruins.

                       "Arbeit

macht frei." Ashes, ashes,
we all fall down.

2. *What is wrong with this picture?*

Here are the famous Medieval cathedrals,
        stone on stone on stone, just
          as history books show them to be.
Here is the new stained glass by Chagall.

Here, unobtrusive, the flat-faced, modern
        city apartments, their uniform
          windows that open two ways. As always,
the ancient clock on the village town hall.

Here are the temples, the synagogues, gold
        domes shining—modern, the architects'
          vision, preserving what's old.
Here are the guards, outside of the walls.

Here is the Römerplatz, *Fachwerk*ed again,
        beguiling, surrounding the central fountain,
          cups and glasses clinking; in winter
the Christmas market, hot *Glühwein*, bright stalls.

Here, the new bright clusters of poppies:
        every village roof-tile, a blossom.

Winding streets, their floods of geraniums.
Each house with its fresh, whitewashed wall.

Here, wide-open, the fields for Sunday
      walks, year-round, so green, the forests
      so carefully tended, the vineyards.
Nowhere, nowhere, did anyone fall.

Here are the camps, open to tourists.
      Green wreaths on the train station wall.
      The names of those who took those trains.
The attempts to remember them all.

Here, the monuments.
There, the monuments.
Everywhere, the open acknowledgment.
What other absence dares sit on my heart?

3.

How dare I write this poem?

4.

"Saatfrüchte sollen nicht vermahlen werden"

Johann Wolfgang von Goethe

Father of Jürgen, lost
wherever your submarine went down:
your son has become an architect, working his way
up, from stage one. If only you could see his own home,
angled just so, so the sun, precisely at noon, will shine
through one small window: high, high, just under the roof.

Father of Olivia, lost
who knows where: your daughter's
a teacher, she can't forget finding, when she
was twenty, your photo, your *Wehrmacht* uniform (so it
was true!), your parents, insisting the ending was wrong.
When she can, she asks poets and Jews to speak at her school.

Father of Volker (professor of
Geography): he learned at twelve you fell
with the SS in Hungary. Every Sunday the family
dinner: the East German question, your absence everyone
skirted around. He's taken a photo of where you fell, a flower.
He speaks this line from a poem: *What we seek for has no place.*

Fathers whose names must not be spoken
Fathers we don't know how to mourn
Fathers who may not be in Heaven
Fathers who didn't come home

Father who did, who lived,
for your son's first six years, behind bars
of a Russian prison camp, your son—named for your
best friend shot down over England—your son has become
a pastor, the father of four, a concert organist. Big man.
Jolly man. All his life he has hated his name.

5.

And here is my betrayal, my shame:

Last summer, in Norway, nearly
everyone I met was delighted: "Ingrid,
that's a Norwegian name!"

"Yes," at first I said, "it is.
But really, I'm German, I'm named for
Ingeborg, my German-Chilean cousin."

"Yes," I learned
to say. "Ingrid *is*
a Norwegian name.

6.

How does memory exist without blame?

7.

After all has been written
After all we have seen in movies, endlessly on tv, and still, wherever we walk,
unexpected, the land mines:

Kloster Arnsburg: unmarked, the graves of the 88 massacred
we didn't know lay right beneath the green of the courtyard.
All afternoon, under umbrellas, dodging puddles, we'd looked
for the oldest Medieval gravestone the guidebook said was there.

(Panzer factory prison workers, in transit to Buchenwald—just ahead
of the Allies, the end of the war, the fleeing Gestapo.
It was simpler to shoot them.)

Ourselves: Americans, all afternoon, under umbrellas,
dodging puddles, we'd looked for the oldest Medieval gravestone
the guidebook said was there.

We thought we were looking for History.
We were trying to keep our shoes dry.

8.

Mother of my new friend in Munich
(the traveling veterinarian, working for peace
between Arabs and Jews; member of SERVAS,
who took us–strangers–into her home, showing us–
first thing–your video, serving us tea before leading the way to
the best Bavarian restaurant, trusting us with her own apartment key)

Mother of yet another daughter
(whose sculptures in concrete capture the body's
memory—*Sand and water themselves are beautiful, they
can't help what we do to them; we must revise the forms we find
them in; what we are given, these cast off things must have aesthetic ends—
small, small changes no one notices. The body knows what they are, it sees*)

Mother with your back
to the camera—haloed, your short, dark hair—
framed by the window—you returned from Auschwitz,
the only one of twenty? more? to raise these children, to lead
tours of Dachau, your voice in this film the voice that has seen everything,
patiently guiding: *The branch stuck into ground will flower again, but it has no roots*

9.

And how do you in your country still
ignore the American Indian question. Unfinished,
the grief of Vietnam. How much memory

can we claim for our own?
My father's parents were German.
My mother's were German. Who can bear to belong

to a country, a whole generation whose fathers, whose mothers,
oneself with the whole world agrees
were wrong?

Nothing is worse than what the other
has done. Who showed no mercy
deserve none.

Atone, atone, who can ever atone?

10. Berlin Tour, 1995

Do you know the stone horses of Turin? One forefoot down, one up, the hero was wounded in battle. Both forefeet down, he came back safely. Both feet up, he died.

—Fedora Giordano

Let us study the monuments
Let us never forget our wrongs
> There, on the Ku-damm, the broken cathedral
> The steeple we pledge we'll never rebuild
> Dark, this lighthouse: eternal dark beacon

Let us praise those who keep faith with stone

Let us praise these monuments
Let us remember the meaning of valor
> Lightning-rod-pointed helmets, or armor
> This nineteenth-century Victory Column
> The Brandenburg Gate, with the horses still flying

Let us sing thanks for all we have won

Let us sing monuments
Let us tell Where things happened: There,
> The "Teacher's Home" for those who taught
> Their leader was wrong; There, a statue of bronze, where

Five who had spoken of killing him, fell
Let our speech fill the echoing silence

Let us speak monuments
Let us say art will transform it all
      Totally covered, the Reichstag shimmering, paid for with fabric
      Scraps and drawings, Jürgen has bought one, has gone to Berlin;
      The people had picnics, all day, all night, on the Reichstag lawn
Let us revisit the scene of our scorn

Let us revisit monuments
Let us enter the dark of the stone: in stark
      Relief, within the former unknown soldier's tomb
      Within one beam: Kollwitz' mother folded around
      The hope of all the world's mothers, dead in her arms
Let us learn to let ourselves mourn

11.

How long does this go on? What river ends at the sea?

12.

When they brought her to me and she first
opened her eyes, I thought I never had seen such blue.
Blue of the sea, storm clouds gathering, deep
Wedgewood, Slate,
Indigo blue.
         They'll change
soon enough,
the nurse soon informed me,
most babies have such eyes when they're born.

When they brought your baby to you,
had you
ever seen such blue?

And you? And you?

13.   *50 Years of Peace: 8 May 1945–8 May 1995*

"From Many Wounds You Bleed, O People"
— Käthe Kollwitz

Even before May, it begins:
in Schwerin, the Kollwitz *Ausstellung* we find
after New Year's, a retrospective of all
her life's conscience

In Frankfurt, the installation
we find between acts of the *Dreigoschen Oper*:
papier-mâché prisoners, uniforms, plates, cups, the tools
of torture (*50 Jahre Befreiung von Auschwitz-Birkenau*), cellbars
spilling into the lobby, no way around them

In Frankfurt, the Jewish Museum's
Rothchild exhibit; the *Literaturhaus* lectures: *Kinder in Auschwitz*;
Überleben im Lager?; the photos: *Auschwitz 1994*; the photo exhibit: *"Now."*

Berlin: *50 Jahre Frieden in Deutschland*: 88 pages, edged in black:
month by month the field trips, the speeches, concurrent exhibits:

Festspielgalerie; Academie der Künste; Amerika-Gedenkbibliothek;
the *Deutsches Historisches Museum;* the *Anti-Kriegs-Museum; Museum für
Verkehr und Technik; Schwules Museum.*

In Frankfurt, in Jena: Britten's "War Requiem."
Brahms', in Jena; Berlin.

Just this one year, a friend predicts. Then life will go on.
Friend, I know a Sabine, in Jena,
daughter of Peter and Rosemarie.
She's named her daughter "Sarah."

Sarah's playmates are Reuben,
Benjamin, Aaron, Hannah. Like Sarah,
they're pink-cheeked and blonde.

14. *Across the River: The Gift*

You sit in the midst of immense love, not alone.

—Marilyn Krysl

After the newsreels
After LIFE photographers gave us the scenes of carnage
Disembodied, still, the hand on the fence in the
Mind's eye: who took it down? And then?

Here in France: unexpected, above the town of Bergheim,
This graveyard of German fallen that surely, we said,
Would be overgrown, untended such a small sign near the inn
Where we stayed; among vineyards, such a small town)

This whole green dome of the hill trimmed with stone:
A perfect geometry I walk among, reading the names, the dates,
Three deep: Hans, twenty-four; Günther, eighteen; and this one
And this, his name, his age, unknown, and each: one

Of more than five thousand brought here together
By children of children of those whom German fire
Brought down, strangers still tending to those for whom
Mothers mourned, to whose graves they could not come,

Who could have been my own young father, his body
The broken wing of worship gone wrong. Oh, it's Abraham
All over again, it's Isaac, and where was the angel? Unforeseen,
On page after page, *My friend*, this book in the Visitor's Room,

In hands of brothers, daughters, sons, *My father*: Oh Prodigal
Love, these names out of hiding, multitudes ahead of my own,
The fields of your memory forever mined with futility: Oh
Exiled Tears springing, stinging, impossible. Yours. My own.

IV.

"MEMORY/MEMORIAL":
THEME AND VARIATIONS

Part of the interdisciplinary gallery exhibit titled "Memory/Memorial"

Eugene, Oregon, June 16–27, 1999

For Susi Rosenberg, sculptor

and Ingeborg Kolar, mixed media artist

»»

High above the village of Sankt Goar on the banks of the Rhine
Eight years after my aged father's great German-Chilean heart
Stopped, I stepped where he as a dreamer fifty years
Before had recited Heine's poem of enchantment
And took with me flowers, friends, a poem of
My own about him, which we read aloud
And burned, and I cast the ashes over
The river that never for him saw
Battle, saw shame, and I let
This young father go.   And when my mother
                              Telephones from Tucson to say
                        The family graves in Michigan will be
                  Tended again this year, she's sent a distant
            Cousin a check for geraniums, red as those we
      Always planted every Decoration Day in memory of
   Her own German parents dead before I was born, their
Granite stones my playground, their stillness my truant heart,
She doesn't say *When I am gone* or guess I know her fear. Lord,
How do I live truly and still plant hope with the right, bright word?

To plant, to build, to sew of the cloth of despair something visible.
Shrine. Altar. Pillar. To join, in this ritual, every known legion
Of loss. Look, here is our faith in Forever, forever gone.
Here, the proof our strongest love wasn't enough.
Look, this last grasp at permanence: trusted
Stone holding in view what arms cannot.
Your name. This incomprehensible
Absence. Look, here is myself,
As never before, pleading
No, No, No, No, No.

                                        O, Saint Anthony
                                  Patron of everything lost,
                             Your vocal chords hung behind
                        Glass in the great cathedral of Padova
                     Over your pickled, jeweled, silent tongue,
                 Last year I touched your tomb's green marble,
             The way new friends insisted. My fingertips tingled
         With who knows what if not inexhaustible stored up grief
     And hope. Or was it spirit? Or was it the pulse of every last
Hand before me, burned into stone. Holding me steady, this hum.

»»

And when the loss is not ours alone, when natural laws are turned
Upside down and all the words for *disaster* clang endlessly on
The tongue—what chorus could possibly grow from that
Sound? What song? Each ear tuned to memories
All its own, each absolute absence a horror all
Its own with nothing in common despite
The common bomb, the planned
Extermination, ethnicity, gun,
The vast need to blame
Changing nothing   And where is the myth
                                              To bind us? Where the image
                                         Known the world round to contain
                                      Each shared human grief? You, whose
                                  Mother survived the camps, no other family.
                             You, your father, the doctor, whose enemy U-boat
                        Never surfaced again. And will we allow the names of
                   The parents slain by their son to be inscribed with those of
               Classmates on whom later he turned the gun? In this nation's
          Capitol, our faces mirrored, splintered, on that black, shining wall.

»»

Altar of sacrifice, altar of stones, Abraham's Angel saving the son
Just in time—the measure of Abraham's faith tried and won.
Altar of offerings, altar of wine transubstantiated by time,
By stories of what your father did unto mine, into
Bitterness, flames, blood of the martyrs used
As memory's sustenance, keeping fury
Alive: yours the sweet bodies,
Betrayed once again: you,
Soldiers of the one
True God.   Mountains
                                        Of eyeglass rims,
                                   Mountains of shoes,
                              Ovens, train tracks, rusted
                         Where once they were used but
                    No one place where those who seek
               Can light a candle, no gravestone, no shrine
          To mark the exact place of death that will never be
     Known, body never found, as waves cover those drowned
At sea. Footsteps, heartbeats: these spaces between are for you.

»»

You whose family four years fled through jungles, whose mother,
Camp by camp, weakened, the cancer left to spread, untreated
You, whose mother fled with her children from Russian invasion
Your train bombed and bombed again as it inched its way south
You whose daughter disappeared on her everyday route home.

You to whom a government gave blankets riddled with smallpox
You whom radiation ravaged, whose fatherland won't remember
You for whom the midnight knock on the door will echo forever
You for whom the syllables Tiananmen, Kent State, still smolder
You whose generation's memory is short

You who cannot bear the sound of movie gunfire, cars' backfires
You who've gathered together severed limbs from the wreckage
The swamp water; you, family whose mourning can never begin
You who never again will look into cameras, you who have seen
More of the face of evil than anything minds can begin to imagine.

You who look for reasons where none exist, who bring to these
Elegies, images of your own, too deep for speech, wave upon
Wave they return when least you expect them, flotsam weighing
The future down. What shape do we give to horror, what form?
Silence between the paving stones of these stanzas: this is for you.

»»

Does your sorrow diminish my sorrow
Can my memory speak for yours
Does one horror extinguish another
Whose grief most worthy of news

Page where memory turns to memorial
Legacy we affirm or deny
Will your austerity silence my song
Will beauty blacken the eye

You who say there is no redemption
You whose path is to reconcile all
You, caught in the wave, in suspension
Whose words would shatter this wall

Does hope ever come from moments of stasis
Where do both sides of the slash converge
The angle of sharpest ascending: the point
The airplane could stall, could plunge

Whose memory becomes memorial
Which edge of the tongue, whose dart
Yesterday's images still patrolling
The borders between our hearts

»»

On the banks of the Lethe we reaped Forgetfulness. By the great
River Jordan we put down our Sins. In the name of the Father,
The Son, we entered still waters, we joined in Covenants,
Bathed in the Ganges, the Nile, the Tigris, Euphrates,
Burned on the stone steps of Benares, our cups
Running over, our souls in Redemption's
Green pastures, comfort always from
The water: What god, what clergy
Could ever have pictured any
River that could not flow.   Out of our cast-
                                      Off materials, out of
                                     Cinders ground to dust,
                                 Out of common lime and clay
                              Fired beyond enduring, then cooling,
                          Then joining together with sand and gravel,
                     This centuries-old conglomeration of syllables, this
                 Musical chord that with the careful addition of moisture,
            Water, will echo louder every passing year. Call it concrete.
       Holy Alchemy! Earth's memory! Returned to you with this song.

»»

Pillar of cloud, pillar of fire, beacon out of yesterday's bondage
Pillar of salt, pillar of stone, counsel not to look back upon
That which cannot be reconciled, never be won, though
We, like Simeon, hungry for words that don't exist
Would fast the rest of our lives atop a pathway
Of pillars, each one higher, higher. Though
We'd journey to the Pillars of Hercules,
Sentries at the void's edge. Though
Like Samson, blinded, raging, we
Would pull the temple down.

Though we also
Could build, seed by
Syllable, image by sound
Cairns of paving stones, ways
To carry history within us, not set it
Down by the water, not cultivate ever-
Lasting blame. Places we've been, those foot-
Steps are in us forever. Shall we not also use them?
Places we're going can't keep the heart from transfiguring.
Pillars, each one cast in the same mold, guiding memory along.

»»

And when the flowers draping the fence have shriveled to brown,
Who is it, unknown to us, takes them all down? And when
Sculptures, altars, completed, must look for new homes?
When the name on the cross at the curve in the road
Can no longer be read, and the hilltop cross over-
Looking our town is replaced by a flag, *More*
Democratic, voters have said, *It speaks for*
Us all. And the *Kalapuya* people, the
Villages standing below this spot?
The reasons why all are gone?   Spring cleaning, again,
                                   At home, the need for ever
                            More room to save all loved ones'
                        Flotsam and Jetsam, as well as our own.
                    Greeting cards, so full of intentional sentiment,
                  How can we throw them away? Clusters of stones
              On the mantel, plucked from days that will never return.
          Flowers Mother has pressed, found in a book. Pocket watch,
      Was it her father's? Her mother's best doily, or was it an aunt's?
    She told you. So you will remember. And you will never be gone.

All the way from Japan the turquoise fishing float journeys, seven
Years of glass bobbing the waves to wash up at last on our beach
A gleaming ball of sun with luck we sometimes find after a storm
The way memory can surface unexpectedly, blinding and vacant of
All but joy: Father's voice, seven years gone, returned in a dream.

And these too reappear: faceless, blameless, words of your mother
With every reason to echo the customary refrain—We must never
Let it happen again—recalling for us, *I had the good fortune of not
Being brutal. Knowing we can be cruel makes peace much more
Dear.* And then the film is over, her voice returned again to space.

And when the darkest day of the year returns to our town, where
Does the heart feel safe? You, whose child left one last kiss on your
Cheek like a scar pulsing each time the news brings yet another
School shooting, the word *tomorrow* forever bordered in black.
Moments of Silence, sweet shimmerings, let us give way to them.

Daily observances, let us build with them, let us make of the days
We're given a celebration of everything that could be taken away.
Spaces between these verses, these are for you, for small gestures

That pass and are gone, like the private kiss I wasn't meant to see:
One who no longer walks on his own, or talks, who, shaking, took
The hand of his wife of thirty years and slowly raised it to his lips.

NOTES

Cover Photo

Susi Rosenberg, "Path I" (detail), 1997. Concrete, rusted steel, particle board, in 12 repeating sections. Feldafing, Germany. Photo by Susi Rosenberg.

Division Pages

I.

Ingeborg Kolar. "Pilgrim's Progress" (side view), 1999. Wood, brass, glass, iron, electric light, 19th-century handpainted lantern slides, in a sequence of 9 wooden "altars," joined by an iron chain. Eugene, Oregon. Photo by Susi Rosenberg.

II.

Susi Rosenberg. "Gestörtes Wachtum: Interrupted Growth," 1997. Rusted iron. Feldafing, Germany. Photo by Susi Rosenberg.

III.

Ingeborg Kolar. "Pilgrim's Progress" (detail), 1999. Wood, brass, glass, iron, electric light, 19th-century handpainted lantern slides, in a sequence of 9 wooden "altars," joined by an iron chain. Eugene, Oregon. Photo by Ingeborg Kolar.

IV.

Susi Rosenberg. "Path II," 1999. Concrete, rusted steel, water, in 12 repeating sections. Eugene, Oregon. Photo by Susi Rosenberg.

"Learning the Mother Tongue"

The first draft of this poem was written during the month of April 1997, while I was in residence, as a guest of the Kulturreferat München, at the Villa Waldberta, Feldafing, Germany. Not technically part of the interdisciplinary artwork "Time: Word: Space," which resulted in the second long poem in this book, this poem began to emerge as the result of issues— and memories—that arose as I worked (in English) on our interdisciplinary project, while continuing my daily study of German. I wish to pay tribute to my German language teacher, Linda Gunn, for her excellent night school class I took for three years in Springfield, Oregon. Seeds for parts of this poem were cast by her.

German Phrases Used in the Poem

Haben Sie ein Kopf, bitte?—Do you have a head, please?

Ja, natürlich, und Sie? —yes, of course, and you?

Denkbar —imaginable, conceivable

Mach schnell—make haste, hurry up

Strewwelpeter—character in children's book of the same title by Dr. Heinrich Hoffmann

Dreh dich rum—turn around

Abgeschiedenheit—solitude, privacy

Wiedersehen—to see again

Wiederaufnameverfahren—retrial, appeal

Kinderfreundsehenlichkeit —(not a word; invented for purposes of this poem)

Bist du ein gutes Mädchen?—Are you a good girl?

Ja, ich bin ein gutes Mädchen.—Yes, I am a good girl.

Text Source:

Hirschfield, Ted. German Requiem: *Poems of the War and the Atonement of a Third Reich Child.* St. Louis, Missouri: Time Being Books, 1993, p. 65.

"Suite for the Spirit's Geometry"

The first draft of this poem was written during the month of April 1997, while I was in residence, as a guest of the Kulturreferat München, at the Villa Waldberta, Feldafing, Germany. Its original function was to serve as the verbal component of the collaborative, interdisciplinary artwork, "Time: Word: Space," created and first shown in the Villa's art studio with two German colleagues, sculptor Susi Rosenberg and painter Traude Linhardt, both of Munich.

Rosenberg's contribution was two large, many-segmented sculptures: "Path I" and "Gestörtes Wachtum: Interrupted Growth," photos of which are represented in this book.

"Path I" consisted of 3 main parts, each of which was repeated 12 times, arranged in a row 30 feet long. These parts consisted of 1) low, semi-circular slabs of poured concrete, equal in shape and size, resting on the floor; 2) single strips of rusted iron, bent in a slight curve, equal in shape and size, placed between the concrete slabs, with one end resting on the floor and the other propped against the topmost section of 3) a pile of thin (1") end-pieces of particle board shelving, each approximately 1 foot square, stacked in piles of ascending heights, to resemble stacks of books.

"Gestörtes Wachtum: Interrupted Growth" consisted of many narrow, irregular lengths of rusted iron, each bent twice, lengthwise (to resemble upside-down train tracks), arranged on the floor in an overlapping and interconnecting pattern to form one large, incomplete circle that appeared, from a distance, like rings of a tree.

I deeply regret that due to an unfortunate lack of reproducible photo documentation, I am not able to include a visual image of Linhardt's striking work, "Time Stations." This piece consisted of 18 panels of clear, polyurethane sheeting (like heavy-duty, clear plastic shower curtains), suspended in three long rows, several feet above the floor, across the width of the studio. Each panel contained words, symbols, patterns and runic designs, in white, light orange, and black acrylic. Panels in rows two and three were visible through the panels of row one. From this perspective, images from all three layers/rows were superimposed.

The poet referred to in this poem is Michael Wüstefeld, of Dresden, Germany.

Other References

"rings of trees," "circle to be broken"—references to Rosenberg's sculpture
   "Interrupted Growth."
"armors made of wax," "grave tokens"—references to Linhardt's earlier works.
"scraps of cloth," "paths between"—references to Linhardt's "Time Stations."
"stone and wood and steel," "turning of the line," "wheel"—references
   to Rosenberg's "Path I."

"Questions of Mercy"

This poem records observations made during my year as Senior Fulbright Professor at the J.W. Goethe Universität, Frankfurt am Main, Germany, 1994-95. I am indebted to the German Fulbright Commission and to Professor Dr. Martin Christadler, Head of the Department of English and American Studies in Frankfurt, for their faith and support. I wish also to thank the German friends, family, and strangers who shared their stories with me. Their spiritual burdens became my own, giving rise to the poems in this book, which began here, with "Questions of Mercy."

The lines by Denise Levertov are from her poem "Life at War," in *The Sorrow Dance*.

Additional Notes

The cartoon is in the book *These Strange German Ways*, by Susan Stern. The original caption is "Reimposing order on chaos." "*Arbeit macht frei*," literally, "Work makes us free," is a slogan from the Nazi concentration/work camps.

"*What is wrong with this picture?*" is the title used for a type of visual game often found in American children's activity books.

"*Saatfrüchte sollen nicht vermahlen werden*": "Seed for the Planting Must Not Be Ground," title of Käthe Kollwitz lithograph, 1942.

The words by Fedora Giordano were spoken in conversation.

"From Many Wounds You Bleed, O People": "*Aus vielen Wunden blutest du, oh   Volk*," title of Kollwitz etching, 1896.

The words by Marilyn Krysl are from her poem "Nammu: To Adam," in *Warscape with Lovers*.

"'Memory/Memorial': Theme and Variations"

The first draft of this poem was written in Eugene, Oregon, in the Spring of 1999, as part of the interdisciplinary gallery exhibit "Memory/Memorial," with sculptor Susi Rosenberg and mixed media artist Ingeborg Kolar. Each artist brought a different yet related perspective to this piece. Rosenberg, from Munich, Germany, is the daughter of an Auschwitz survivor. German-born Ingeborg Kolar, of Corvallis, Oregon, is the daughter of a medical doctor lost at sea in a German submarine. Myself, the American-born daughter of German parents once-removed, who themselves were raised in German-speaking households (in Chile and Michigan), have been cut off from my German heritage for a variety of reasons, not the least of which was my birth during the second world war.

Kolar's contribution, "Pilgrim's Progress," was a series of 9 wall-mounted brass "altars," each depicting a scene from a round, 19th-century, hand colored lantern slide, backlit by candle-style incandescent lamps. Each altar spot was connected by a looped chain, terminating in a rusty, cannonball-like device. Juxtaposing the images from "Pilgrim's Progress" was a stack of first-person narratives collected from hostile events throughout history: narratives of soldiers and their loved ones: wives, sweethearts, and orphaned children. The personal narratives, contrasted by official war statistics, were presented in the form of government-like documents, bound in brass covers, supported by a spotlit, free-standing pedestal in the center of the floor.

Rosenberg's freestanding "Path II" consisted of 78 hand-poured, square, concrete blocks, stacked in twelve progressively taller units, beginning with one block and rising to a unit twelve blocks high. On the top surface of each block, occupying half the space, was a triangular recess that held water, representing a river that does not flow. Between each "stack," and resting on the floor, was a low arch, consisting of two very thin, bent, rusted steel strips, placed one on top of the other. The entire piece—concrete stacks and arches—was approximately 30 feet long.

Additional Notes

My father, Edward J. Wendt (1902–1986), born in Chile, worked in Germany from 1927-1929, on his way to permanent residence in the United States. One of his favorite memories was of a trip to the Loreley, a high cliff above the Rhine River and the seat of a legend, Germany's version of the Greek sirens, immortalized by Heinrich Heine. My mother, Matilda Petzke Wendt (1911-2000), born in Michigan, lived in Tucson, Arizona, when the first draft of this poem was written.

Saint Simeon Stylites (390? –459) was a Syrian ascetic who, in 423, took up residence on a very small platform atop a stone pillar. Over the years he lived on a succession of pillars, each one higher than the one before. His final 30 years of life were spent atop a final pillar

60 feet tall, from which he preached to pilgrims from many countries.

In 1998, the city of Eugene, Oregon, voted to remove from the hill overlooking the downtown area, a large concrete cross which had been surreptitiously erected 20 years before. The losing voters, calling the original cross a "war memorial," campaigned, successfully, to have a large American flag erected in its stead.

Beachcombers in Oregon are sometimes rewarded, after a storm, with finding Japanese glass fishing floats. The voice of Rosenberg's mother appears in the documentary film "Silent Witness," directed by Harriet Wichin. The flowers on the fence were around Thurston High School, Springfield, Oregon, after the May, 1998, cafeteria shooting in which 2 students were killed and 14 wounded.